MILITARY LIFE

Stories and Poems for Children

Written by:

Peggie Brott

Alison Buckholtz

Judy Hissong

Amy Houts

Jennifer Jesseph

Charlene Kochensparger

Julie LaBelle

Christy Lyon

Karen Pavlicin

Donna Portelli

Cindy Shaw

Michelle Tonsmeire

Illustrated by:

Quinette Cook

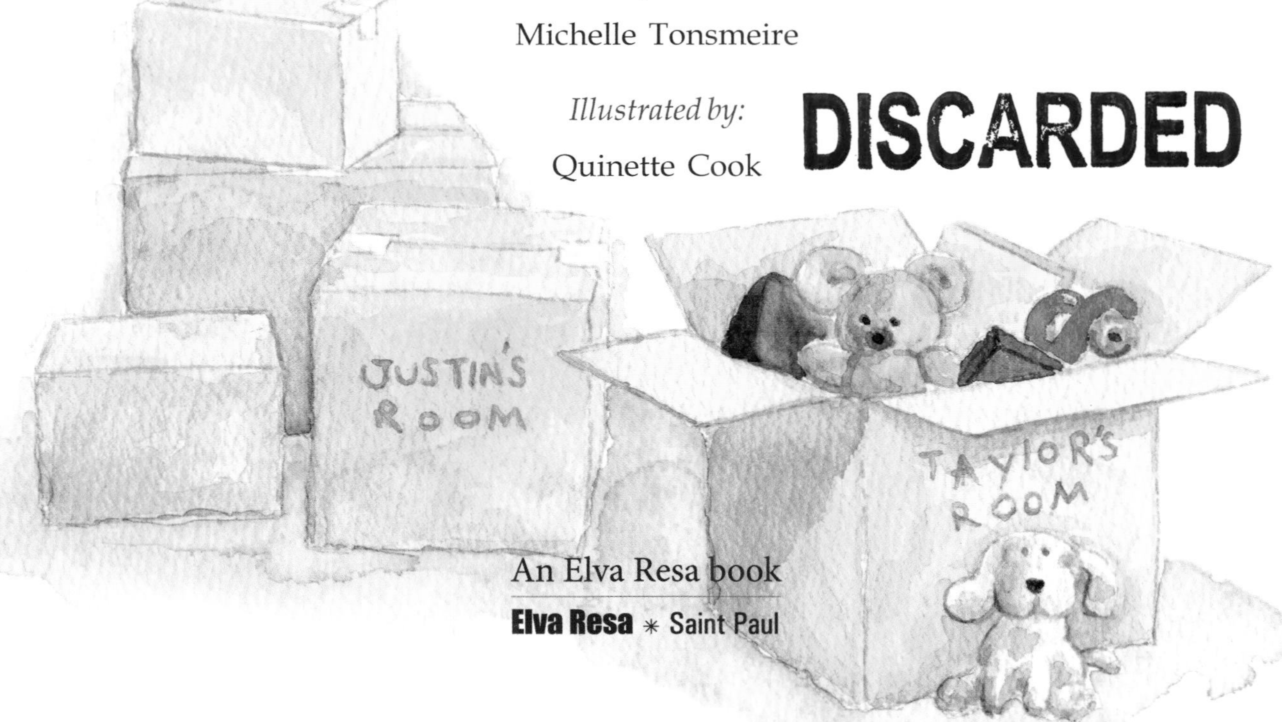

An Elva Resa book

Elva Resa ∗ Saint Paul

Design by Andermax Studios.

ISBN-13: 978-1-934617-09-0

Printed in United States of America.
1 2 3 4 5 6 7 8 9 10

Elva Resa Publishing
8362 Tamarack Vlg, Ste 119-106
St Paul, MN 55125
http://www.elvaresa.com
http://www.militaryfamilybooks.com

MILITARY LIFE
Stories and Poems for Children

Just Like You!

by Julie LaBelle

When you sleep in a tent
And wake up at dawn
Starting your day
With a great big yawn

So can I!

When you stand at attention
Back straight and tall
Eyes straight ahead
Trying hard not to fall

So can I!

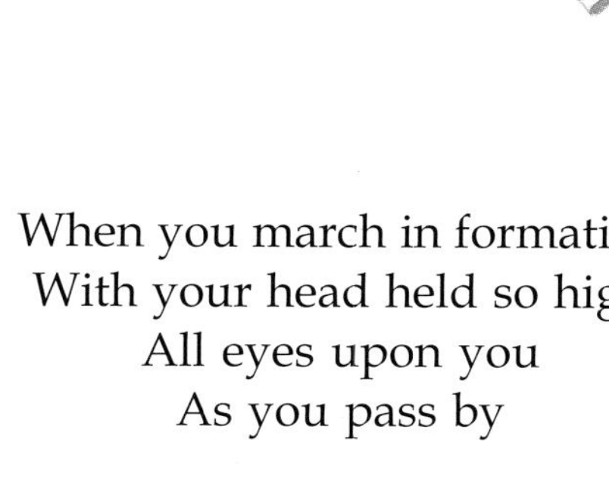

When you march in formation
With your head held so high
All eyes upon you
As you pass by

So can I!

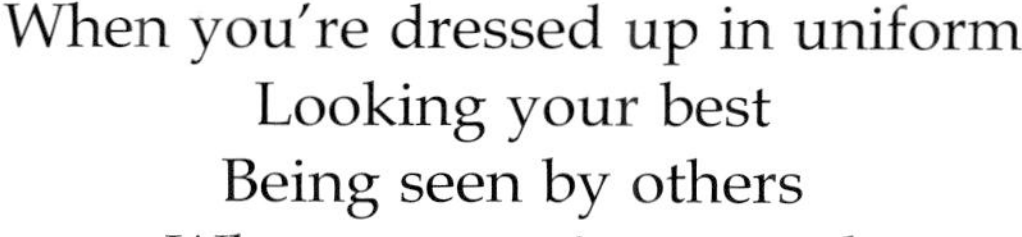

When you're dressed up in uniform
Looking your best
Being seen by others
Who are very impressed

So can I!

When saluting the flag
Hand held to head
Face calm and still
Eyes straight ahead

So can I!

When you run a long way
With a pack on your back
As fast as you can
Without looking back

So can I!

When you do chin-ups and push-ups
And jumping jacks
Building up muscles
You rarely relax

So can I!

When you paint your face
And sit in a tree
Watching closely
For an enemy

So can I!

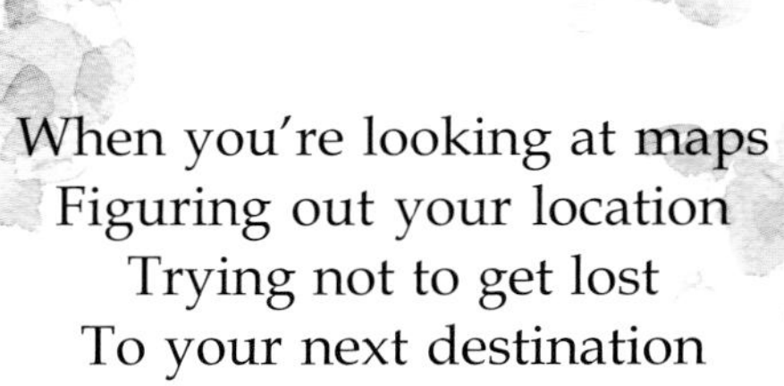

When you're looking at maps
Figuring out your location
Trying not to get lost
To your next destination

So can I!

When you crawl through the mud
On your elbows and knees
Climbing around in bushes and trees
Hoping you don't see snakes or fleas

So can I!

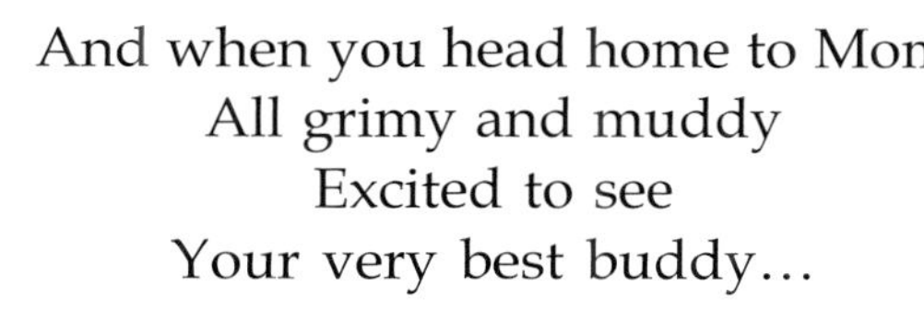

And when you head home to Mom
All grimy and muddy
Excited to see
Your very best buddy...

So can I!

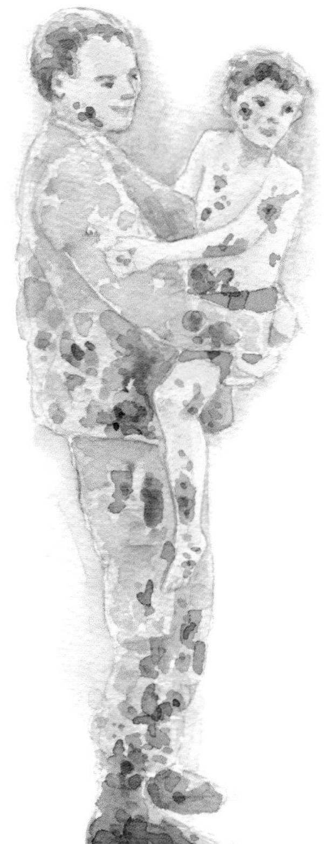

My Space

by Donna Portelli

No matter where I've been or go, this is my favorite place,
A special place just for me that I call *my space.*
Where I can play for hours pretending anything,
I can laugh, cry, make silly sounds, or even loudly sing.
I can sit on my bed and remember all my dreams
Of faraway lands and treasure hunting schemes.

I know that when I close my eyes—wherever that might be—
I'll wake up in my own bed with treasures next to me,
Like photos of my mom and dad, and trophies just a few,
A card from Grandma and some pictures that I drew,
The books I've read a million times and will read a million more,
My foamy ball and basketball hoop hanging on my door,

A little frame I made with Mom on a rainy day,
The wooden cross on the wall to help me when I pray,
My stuffed animal babies I've had since I was small,
The pencil marks Dad made to show I'm growing tall,
Some seashells I collected and put into a jar,
An American flag proudly boasting each and every star.

Right now the walls are painted blue, to look just like the sky.
Next time, maybe I'll change it—I think green is what I'll try.
My blanket's always soft and my pillow's the perfect fit;
My little angel nightlight shines so brightly when it's lit.
Even if we move, or my room I have to share.
As long as I have my space I won't really care.

Bigger or smaller or just the same size, it doesn't matter much
'Cause in my space, I'm in charge of all that I can touch.
Outside the door of my space, things may be different and new:
The house, the yard, the street, or town—these all might change, too.
But no matter where my house might be, even in a different place,
I'll always have my treasures in my new most favorite space.

7
10

Best Friends

by Judy Hissong

I decided I would never again have a best friend
Because I hate goodbyes
Until now I stuck to that

We met the first day of school
I was lost in that big building
You showed me the way to my classroom

My teacher looked like President Lincoln
I was scared and you told me not to be
So I wasn't

You were on my soccer team
Running fast, kicking hard, me too
We cheered when we won
And cheered each other up when we lost

We were shooting baskets outside
When that bird pooped on your face
We laughed until our sides ached
So did your mom

You helped me through some tough times
We laughed through some good times
Math class, playing sports, eating ice cream
We became best friends

I know I'll make new friends again
In each new place I live
None will take your place though
You'll always be my special friend

Goodbye is just a phrase we say
Until we meet again
Thanks for reminding me that
It's always worth the effort to have a best friend

My Daddy Jumps Today

by Michelle Tonsmeire

Today is the day
Have you heard the news?
My daddy jumps today
With a big parachute!

He jumps from a plane
High up in the sky
With other paratroopers
Close by his side.

First, he's off to the airfield
To load up on the plane.
The jumpmaster checks his chute
And sends him on his way.

He boards the plane with other troopers
And stands to one side,
Until the jumpmaster calls to "Hook up!"
All the static lines.

"Green light, Go!
Green light, GO!"
Troopers start to jump—
All their gear in tow.

When Daddy is next
He steps to the door and leaps
Out into the big blue sky
With clouds piled deep.

He counts to 4,000
With his chin upon his chest,
And bends at his waist to see
The country he loves best.

He pulls on his risers
To steer his chute down.
He floats to the drop zone
And PLFs on the ground.

(A "PLF" is
A Parachute Landing Fall.
It's a special way to land
That doesn't hurt at all!)

My daddy jumped today,
And I know it is true—
My daddy loves to jump
With a big parachute!

AIRBORNE ALL THE WAY!

Mama's Been Called Up

by Charlene Kochensparger

SLAM! I push the car door shut so hard it almost breaks the window. It feels good for a second, then I drag my backpack up the stairs to school.

Mama walks me to the door. She has a meeting today and is wearing her dress uniform. I usually tell her she looks awesome in it. Today I don't say anything.

We get to Room 6 and I look at Mama and go in. I do not say, "See you later, alligator."

Mama says, "After awhile, crocodile," anyway.

My teacher Mrs. Sipos says, "Good morning, Kaylee." I stick out my tongue and her eyebrows jump up.

Mama and Mrs. Sipos are talking. I know what they're saying. My mama's been called up and I'm in a snit. Mama says that's when I start slamming doors.

Called up is when your mom or dad has to go away when their military unit is needed. My mama is in the Air Force Reserves. She's going someplace I've never been. Someplace she's never been. Someplace halfway across the world.

Rachel, a girl in my class, walks over to me.

"You in trouble?" she asks.

"I guess," I say. "I stuck out my tongue at Mrs. Sipos."

Rachel giggles and her ponytail bounces. I smile a tiny smile, but then I frown again because I remember.

"What's the matter?" Rachel asks.

"My mama's been called up."

Rachel's brown eyes are serious. "My daddy's been deployed. He's in the Air Force and he's going to be away for a year." She twirls her hair.

I look over and see my teacher still talking with Mama.

"Your mom's pretty," Rachel says.

"And smart," I add, "She's a doctor and works in an office."

"My daddy's a pilot," Rachel says. "We live on base and we always get to have breakfast together. But not now. Not when he's deployed."

"Yeah. Me and Daddy get to see Mama most every night for supper. I won't get to see her for a long time. She'll miss a whole summer of swimming and picnics! It makes me so mad."

Rachel nods. "Daddy will miss my birthday. It's July 15th. It's really sad because he loves cake."

I put my arm around Rachel's shoulders. "It is sad," I agree.

When Mama picks me up after school, she's wearing her old jeans.

"I bought some red and white impatiens to plant," she says. "Want to help?"

She knows I like dirt, but I shrug.

"Okay," she says. "Let's get home and get started."

I'm on watering can duty. I'm very good at watering, but today I'm feeling grumpy about helping. Mama points.

"This flower needs water."

I stomp over and pour water on it.

"Hey! Don't drown him."

"Mama," I say, "it's not a 'him'—it's just an it."

"Hmm," she says, digging some more.

I just stand there. Mama points to the new plant. It's bright red. I drown it too.

Mama digs her next hole and says, "The Air Force needs me. It's important."

"*I'm* important."

Mama says, "Of course you are, but someone has to go."

"Someone *else* should go."

"A lot of people have to go."

"Rachel's daddy has to," I tell her. Mama hands me the little shovel. "Rachel told me he's going to miss her birthday," I say, and kneel down to dig. "Can I buy her a birthday present?"

Mama pushes the flower in the hole I made. "That would be nice."

"Rachel is really going to miss her daddy," I tell her.

Mama stops digging to look at me. She says, "I bet she will, but they must need him, just like they need me."

I know it's important. I know they need doctors. I know my mama's the best. I sigh and drizzle the new plant with water.

"You'll probably help bazillions of people."

Mama laughs. "Not so many, but some, I hope, if they need me."

She stands, puts a finger under my chin and gently lifts it so I have to look at her. "If I could choose, Kaylee, I'd stay right here with you."

"You would?" I ask in a whisper.

She nods.

"Will you miss me?" I ask.

She nods again, but doesn't say anything. I see tears in her eyes and soon they're spilling out.

"Me too," I say, and we squeeze each other so tight it's hard to breathe. "It's okay, Mama. Don't worry."

Mama takes my hand and we walk to the back yard.

"I won't worry. You shouldn't either, because your daddy will be here. He'll make you supper and read you bedtime stories and take good care of you, just like always."

"But Mama, he can't fix my hair for school."

She gives me a little smile. "He's not too good at that, is he?"

I shake my head no.

"We can teach him pigtails and braids before I go."

"Okay," I say. "Mama?" I'm afraid, but I need to know. "Will you get hurt?"

Mama takes a deep breath. She leads me to our swing—the one big enough for all of us, Daddy, Mama and me—and we sit. She puts her arm around me.

"The Air Force trains us to do our jobs and to be safe."

I watch a bee sitting on a tiny white clover. The flower bends over 'cause he's too heavy. "What if you get hurt anyway?"

"Well, if I did need help, there are other doctors to take care of me. But I don't think that will happen. I'm very careful."

"You'll be careful every minute?"

Mama kisses my forehead. "Every minute."

"Promise?" I can't help asking.

"I promise," she says and kisses my cheek. "I promise." She kisses my nose. "I promise." She kisses my chin. "I PROMISE!" She kisses my neck until I laugh.

"Stop! Tickling!" I yell between laughs.

She stops and hugs me again. "I love you, sweetie."

"I love you, Mama, so, so much."

"Still mad?"

"A little bit," I tell her.

"That's okay."

"Good," I say. "I'm probably going to be a little bit mad 'til you get back."

"Don't tell the Air Force," she whispers, "but me too."

"Mama?"

"Yes?"

"Don't stick your tongue out at your commanding officer."

Saying Goodbye

by Peggie Brott

I ran my hand along all the gray and green bags my dad stacked near the front door. His ruck sack and duffel bags were bursting at the seams. Everything he would need for the next twelve months was packed tightly in those bags. Boots, uniforms, a canteen, a flashlight, towels, his shaving kit, and lots of things I didn't even understand how to use. I wondered if I could fit in there, too.

Just two days ago, I sat on the living room floor with my dad. He was spreading out all his gear double checking his list to make sure he had everything. He called out "Four pairs of boots?" I counted them and said, "Check! But why do you need four pairs of boots?"

"I will do a lot of walking where I'm going. My boots will wear out and I'll need a backup pair," he told me.

"Will you walk all over the desert, Daddy?" I asked.

"No," he answered, "I'm going to a city that looks a little bit like the one we live in. There are big buildings, schools, stores, and hospitals. I will walk around the city making sure the people are safe."

"Like a police officer?"

"Yes, Squirt, kind of like a police officer."

Then I wondered why they would need my dad to travel all that way to protect their city. "Daddy? Why can't their own police officers keep them safe?"

"They can, Squirt. But sometimes they need a little extra help, so I'm going to help them. There are kids just like you who live there, and I want to make sure they can play safely in the streets just like you can. Okay?"

That didn't make me feel any better, but I said okay.

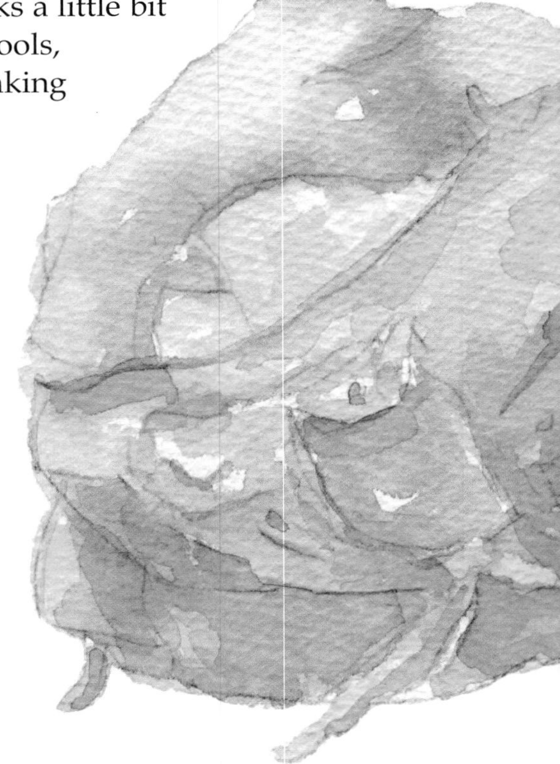

I was standing there staring at my dad's bags, thinking about helping him pack when I remembered the picture I drew him. Did he have enough room to pack it? I ran into the kitchen where I could hear Mom and Dad talking. Dad's voice sounded sad, and Mom was crying. I didn't want to see her cry because then I would cry.

"What's up?" Mom asked, wiping her nose with a tissue.

"Oh, nothing." I decided to ask about the picture later.

I left the kitchen and went to play with my brother in his room. Justin was only two and didn't understand that Dad was going away for a long time. He was playing with his trucks. I felt mad that Justin was so happy. I wanted him to understand and be sad, too.

"Hey, Squirt!" I heard my dad call from the living room. I ran out to see him, and when I got there he was sitting on the floor with a wooden box in his hands. "I have a present for you before I go."

The box looked like a small jewelry box with an American flag painted on top. Daddy opened it and picked up a yellow bracelet and put it on my wrist. "Yellow means you're waiting for someone to come home. Wear this every day until I get home, okay?"

"Yes, Daddy," I said.

Next, he handed me a necklace that looked just like the dog tags he wears. "Read what it says," he told me.

"Daddy loves his little squirt" I read to myself. Then I put it on and gave him a hug. I felt a big lump in my throat and I knew that if I tried to talk that lump would get in the way.

The next thing he took out of the box was a small photo album. "Your mom helped me with this one," he said as he flipped through the pages. Each page had a picture of me and my dad, some words, and some neat looking stickers. "Mom made one for me to take over there, too. So I'll have lots of pictures of you and Justin to keep me company. Now I have one more thing to show you. See the mirror on the inside of this box? This is so you can send me a smile every day. Can you do that?"

The lump in my throat was much bigger, and I knew that I wouldn't be able to stop the tears I'd been fighting back all day. "Yes, I can do that, Daddy," I told him. Then I started to cry.

Dad held me for a long time until we heard Mom say, "Time to go." Dad got up and went to Justin's room. When he came back he was carrying Justin, and Justin was carrying a plastic baby-proof photo album. Dad smiled and said, "Now you two can look at your albums together!" I just nodded because I didn't want to cry again.

Mom and Dad loaded all of his bags in the back of the car. We were going to drive Dad to the buses that would take him and the other soldiers to the airport. Dad had to fly over an ocean to get where he was going. Mom said it would take almost a day for him to get there.

When we got to the buses I saw a lot of people waiting. Some had big signs saying "We'll miss you!" and others were holding American flags. There were kids hugging their dads, wives hugging their husbands, and moms hugging their sons. It made me sad to think of all these soldiers going away and their families missing them. But I remembered they had an important job to do, and that it took special people to do it. I was proud that my dad was one of them.

A soldier came and told my dad it was time to load up the buses. Tears were coming down my mom's face. Mom and Dad hugged and kissed and said "I love you" a bunch of times. Then Dad got down on one knee and looked at me. He had tears in his eyes. I'd never seen my dad cry before. We hugged and gave wet, teary kisses. I didn't want to cry, but the tears came fast and hot. Dad also gave hugs and kisses to Justin and told him not to grow up too much while he was gone.

Justin's
Photos

We watched Daddy walk slowly to the bus. All the soldiers moved slowly. It probably hurt them to say goodbye, too. When Dad was on the bus he opened his window and waved at us. We all waved back and I could hear Justin saying, "Bye bye DaDa!" in an excited voice. How could Justin be excited right now? Why couldn't he understand this wasn't fun?

Suddenly I remembered the picture I made Daddy. I never got to ask if he packed it. I ran up to the bus and could hear my mom call my name, but I didn't slow down. When I got to the bus Dad peeked out his window again and said "Hey, Squirt! What's the matter?"

"Did you bring the picture I drew for you?" I asked.

He patted the front pocket on his uniform. "Right here, next to my heart," he said. He smiled at me and said goodbye again.

I said goodbye and blew him a kiss. "One for the road," I told him.

The buses started up and slowly one pulled out after another. My mom talked with some of the other families, and we all stood there until long after the buses were gone. Some of the kids were playing tag, but I didn't want to play with them. I sat on a curb near our car and drew pictures in a pile of sand. At last my mom said it was time to go home.

That night in my room I sat on my bed with my box on my lap. I still had the necklace and the bracelet on. I turned the box over in my hands, looking at it from every angle. "That's mighty fine craftsmanship," I said, pretending to talk like my dad. I opened the lid and practiced the smile I wanted to send to him when he finally got over there. I practiced a few different smiles until I found one that made my eyes sparkle.

Mom came in and sat on the bed next to me and said, "We'll both miss Daddy, won't we?" I nodded my head yes. She gave me a hug and a kiss on the top of my head. She said she had lots of big plans to keep us busy while Dad was gone. She told me about a trip she was planning to Grandma and Grandpa's house and said she was already thinking about my birthday party in three months.

I sat there for a while after Mom left my room, thinking of all the fun we could have even if Dad wouldn't be here to share it with us. I picked up the small photo album and thumbed through it. There was a picture of my dad holding me when I was just born. He had what Mom would call an "ear-to-ear grin" on his face. Mom had written, "Proud New Daddy" in her best hand writing. That's when it hit me: Mom will have to be both mom and dad while Daddy's gone. She'll have a tough job, too. Hmm… I bet I can come up with all sorts of ways to help her. I grabbed a notebook off my dresser and started to make a checklist, just like the one Dad used before he left.

Start care package for Daddy. Check!
Keep my room neat. Check!
Help Justin play with his trucks. Check!
Send another smile to Daddy. Check!

The Good Day

by Alison Buckholtz

My dad is away.
He's away for a long time.
I can't even count that high.
I can count to 20.
I can count to 10 in Spanish, too.
Mom always smiles when I do that.

Uno
Dos
Tres
Cuatro
Cinco
Seis
Siete
Ocho
Nueve
Diez

Dad's gold car is in the driveway, so sometimes I forget he's not here.
I run in saying, "Daddy!"
Mom says, "We're going to take this one day at a time."
At night, she says, "Today was a good day."
It was a good day for me, too.
Alan shared his squishy frog with me.
When I squeeze it, it lights up.

Dad is on a big boat. It's called an aircraft carrier.
I went on the boat with him before it sailed away on the water.
He picked me up to help me climb the tall, tall ladders.
He showed me his room.
It had a bunk bed, just like mine!
We both sleep on the bottom bunk.

Every week, we send a letter to Dad.
Mom helps me write about my good days.
Here is what I wrote.

Dear Dad,

I had a good day today!

1. I played with a purple balloon.
2. Mom gave me stickers because I ate all my dinner.
3. We sang lots of silly songs and played silly music after Tiny Baby went to bed.

Love,
Me

Sometimes I have to turn a sad day into a good day.
Like when I see Dad's picture on the wall.
Tiny Baby always yells "Da Da!" and tries to touch it.
I never yell "Da Da."
But I think it.
Then I want Dad to come home.
On those days, I tell Mom, "I want Daddy!"
Sometimes I cry.

On those days, Mom holds me on the couch.
She tells me that Dad has a picture with him all the time.
It's the picture of us standing under a giant fountain.
We're both smiling and we are wet and shiny.
Dad kisses the picture of me every night when he goes to sleep.

Mom says Dad wishes he could be here so we could play together.
Mom takes out crayons and paper.
We draw pictures of Dad and me playing together.
That's how a sad day turns into a good day.

Mom, Tiny Baby, and I have some sad times while Dad is away
because we miss Dad and we love him very, very much.
We have lots of good days, too.
We mark them off on the calendar.
The days fly by like little birds.

Now, Dad's big boat is sailing through the ocean.
Toward me!
He is coming home soon.
"Not today," Mom says. "Not tomorrow. But soon."
When soon comes, I will get back from school and run in the house.
I'll yell, "Daddy!"

On that day, Dad will be home.
He will run to me and hold me high in the sky.
We will sit on the couch together for a long time.
That won't just be a good day.
That will be the best day of all.

Holding Mom's Kite

by Jennifer Jesseph

Dear Mom,
When you deployed,
I imagined you as a kite, flying
so high and far away we lost sight,
but we feel you tug
the string. Do you
feel us tug too?
Dad, Danny,
and I
hold
the string. Every day we wind one r

you are one day closer. We are here pulling you home with our LOVE!!!

When Mommy Comes Home

by Amy Houts

When Mommy comes home,
I will watch at the window
and be the first to shout,
"Mommy's home!"

When Mommy comes home,
I will whisper my secrets
so only Mommy can hear,
that my new friend is Megan,
my pet turtle died,
and my teacher, last week, had a new baby girl.

When Mommy comes home,
I will say, "Look at me! I have changed.
I am taller! Do you see?"
And Mommy will say, "Look at you! You have grown!"

She will hug me and kiss me and hold me so tight.
Mommy will twirl me,
and we'll dance in a circle.
When we're dizzy we'll stop
and fall on the ground.

Mommy will say, "I'm so glad to be home!
I have missed you so much!"
I will help her unpack,
march in her boots,
and try on her hat.

Mommy will laugh and take out her camera.
I will look like a soldier, just like my mom.
Then Daddy and I will go into the kitchen,
and watch Mommy smile
because Daddy and I are cooking for her.

Then Mommy will say, "It's time for a bath."
She'll draw hearts on the mirror
while I'm splashing around.

When it's time for bed, she will read me a story,
and sing to me softly as I close my eyes.
She will pull up the covers under my chin
and tuck me in tight.
And whisper her love in the words of a prayer.

That's what will happen
when Mommy comes home.

When Daddy Comes Home

by Amy Houts

When Daddy comes home
I will race out the door
and stand at attention, give my salute,
and then a high five.

When Daddy comes home
I will jump in his arms
and he'll hold me up high.
I'll pretend I'm an airplane
looking down on the world.

When Daddy comes home
I will put on his hat
and climb on his back
and Daddy will carry me into the house.

When Daddy comes home
he will say, "How's my boy?"
I will say, "Look at me! I am stronger! Do you see?"

Then we'll wrestle in fun.
First he'll pin me down, and then let me win.
We'll rest on the couch, with Mommy beside us.

I will climb on Dad's lap
and look at his ribbons,
and he will explain what each of them means.

And when it is late, he will say, "Time for bed."
He will read me a story,
and sing to me softly as I close my eyes.
He will pull up the covers under my chin
and tuck me in tight
And whisper his love in the words of a prayer.

That's what will happen
when Daddy comes home.

Love Letters

by Karen Pavlicin

Each day my mom writes a love letter.
When Dad's away she writes
"I miss you" and "I love you"
and mushy stuff like that.

Sometimes she puts notes in my lunchbox.
"You are my sunshine."
"UR special 2 me."
"The world is brighter because of you."

I asked Mom how she can think of
so many things to write.
She said her heart tells her what to say.

Dad writes love letters, too.
He leaves Mom Post-It notes
on the mirror or in a drawer.
"Your smile is beautiful."
"You're the best." "Need milk."

So one day on my own I thought of all the ways
I love my mom and dad.
I wrote them on little pieces of paper
and put them in a treasure box.

"I love when you sing to me."
"You give the best hugs."
"Your hands are soft." "Your hair smells good."
"I love you to the moon and back."

"I love the way you write love letters every day."

It's Five O'Clock

by Cindy Shaw

A booming blast from the cannon's mouth.
Then the bugle's noble notes march out.
So triumphant.

It's five o'clock.

Racing outside, before it can start,
I place my right hand over my heart.
My eyes find it.

I watch the Colors shining so true,
Proudly waving to me and to you.
Red, white, and blue.

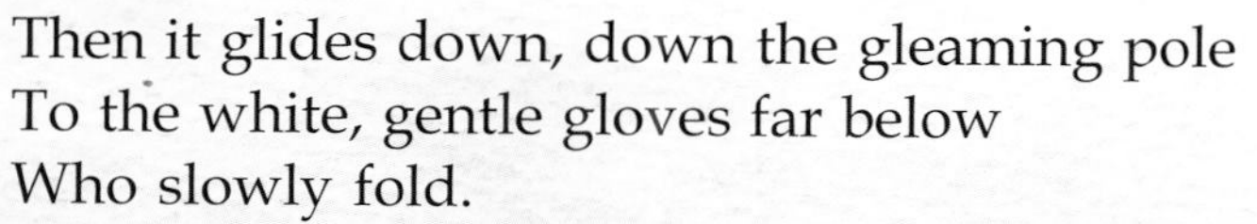

Then it glides down, down the gleaming pole
To the white, gentle gloves far below
Who slowly fold.

It's five o'clock.

Beloved banner of liberty,
Our families fight for you each day.
Rest now, I say.

For come tomorrow, yes, it is true,
Faithful flag of our country, you,
Will rise anew.

It's five o'clock.

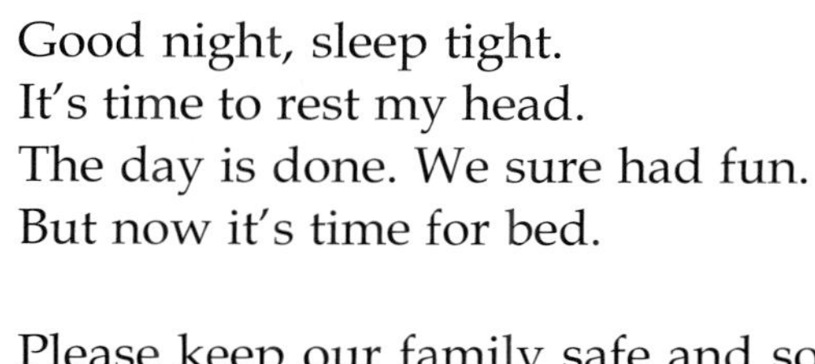

Good Night

by Christy Lyon

Good night, sleep tight.
It's time to rest my head.
The day is done. We sure had fun.
But now it's time for bed.

Please keep our family safe and sound:
Mommy, Daddy, Brother,
Sister, Grandma, Aunt and Uncle,
Grandpa and the others.

Tomorrow the sun'll still shine bright.
The day will start again.
But for now it's time to rest.
And be glad for where we've been.

PEGGIE BROTT believes in helping her three children find the silver lining in any situation and enjoys all the adventures Army life brings. She was inspired to write "Saying Goodbye" during her husband's second deployment.

ALISON BUCKHOLTZ is the author of *Standing By: The Making of an American Military Family in a Time of War.* She wrote "The Good Day" for her children, Ethan and Esther, while her husband, a Navy pilot, was deployed.

JUDY HISSONG moved several times while her dad was in the Army and made many friends along the way. The friendship in her poem "Best Friends" continues today after seven moves and many, many years.

AMY HOUTS, the daughter of an Army tech sergeant, has written 37 books for children. She was inspired to write "When Mommy Comes Home" and "When Daddy Comes Home" after reading about a mother saying goodbye to her young children before deploying.

JENNIFER JESSEPH has been writing poems for more than 20 years. When she thought of parents deploying, the image of a kite came to mind and that's when she wrote "Holding Mom's Kite."

CHARLENE KOCHENSPARGER is a writer who lives near Wright-Patterson Air Force Base with her firefighter husband and two children. "Mama's Been Called Up" was inspired by her children's school librarian who wanted more books about moms who deploy.

JULIE LABELLE's son grew up to be a Marine just like his dad. Their Marine neighbors were also good role models for how to play hard in the mud and get hosed off at the end of the day "Just Like You!"

CHRISTY LYON loves to read to her two boys before bedtime. She wrote "Good Night" to add a prayer for safety and grateful thanksgiving for their day.

KAREN PAVLICIN exchanged more than 800 handwritten letters with her Marine husband during his deployments. She loves to leave love notes in her son's lunchbox and read reminders from her treasure box. It was her son's love note on the pantry door that inspired her to write "Love Letters."

DONNA PORTELLI loves to make a wonderful space for each person in her family. A recent move to a new neighborhood and her daughters' attempts to make their new space their own inspired her poem "My Space."

CINDY SHAW is married to an Army military police officer. They currently live on post next to the parade field. Each evening, their children run out to watch the lowering of the flag, inspiring her poem "It's Five O'Clock."

MICHELLE TONSMEIRE's husband has been in airborne units all over the world. She was inspired to write "My Daddy Jumps Today" the first time their young son watched his daddy jump at the drop zone. Michelle lives in North Carolina with her husband and two children.

QUINETTE COOK, illustrator, lives in Minnesota with her husband, two children, and a Weimaraner named Jazz. She holds a BA in commercial art and design from the University of Minnesota.